Star Power

Star Power

Adapted by Lara Bergen

Based on the series created by Steve Marmel

Part One is based on the episode, "Fast Friends," Written by Michael Feldman & Steve Marmel

Part Two is based on the episode, "Cheater Girls," Written by Dava Savel

Disney PRESS
New York

Printed in the United States of America

First Edition
1 3 5 7 9 10 8 6 4 2
J689-1817-1-10032

Library of Congress Control Number on file.
ISBN 978-1-4231-2277-7

For more Disney Press fun, visit www.disneybooks.com

Visit DisneyChannel.com

PART
ONE

CHAPTER 1

It was lunchtime for the cast and crew of *So Random!*, the number one sketch-comedy show on TV. And it was Monday—which meant one thing: meatball sandwiches for everyone! As usual, Grady Mitchell and Nico Harris, the two male cast members of *So Random!*, were very excited about this.

"These are the greatest sandwiches *ever*," Nico said, reaching for another. He and Grady had brought a whole tray of them back from the cafeteria to enjoy in the privacy of the prop house, the cast's favorite room to hang out in.

"I *love* Meatball Monday!" agreed Grady. As he took a giant bite of his sandwich, tomato sauce splattered everywhere. But Grady just shrugged and continued eating.

Just then, Tawni Hart, the longest-running cast member—and self-proclaimed "star" of the show—walked in. She took one look at Grady and shook her head.

"Here's a little Tawni tip for you," she told them, eyeing the mess that Grady had made. "It's even tastier if some of it lands in your mouth."

Grady crossed his eyes in order to better see the tip of his nose, which was covered in sauce. "Yeah, well, I'm saving this for later," he told Tawni.

"I'd like to see *you* eat one of these sand-wiches and stay clean," Nico added.

Tawni just rolled her eyes. Did she have

to teach other people *everything*?

"It's easy," she said, "if you use Tawni Hart's patented 'bite, wipe, and gloss.'" She picked a sandwich up off the tray and, pinkies in the air, brought it slowly and carefully to her mouth. "Bite . . ." she said, taking a dainty nibble. "Wipe . . ." She took a napkin and dabbed at the tiniest drop of sauce. Satisfied, she crumpled the napkin and carelessly tossed it away. "And *gloss*! Okay, now you try," she said, grabbing some lip gloss from her purse.

Nico and Grady looked at each other. "Bite . . ." they repeated, digging in obediently as sauce dripped out of their sandwiches. "Wipe . . ." Grinning, they smeared the sauce across their mouths with their sleeves. "And sauce!" they finished with a flourish.

Tawni put her head in her hands. They were hopeless. *And* gross!

Just then, Sonny Munroe walked in, looking

much more dressed up than usual.

Sonny was the newest member of the *So Random!* cast. In fact, she'd only recently moved to Hollywood from her hometown in Wisconsin. The whole TV-star thing was new to her, still— and sometimes it was even scary. But it was also a dream come true, and a challenge she was definitely up to.

"Hey, guys," Sonny said, giving a little twirl.

"Have a seat," Nico mumbled through a mouthful of food. "Meatball Monday!"

Sonny looked down at the plate of sloppy sandwiches and shook her head. "I'd love to, but I can't," she said with a grin. She smoothed her hair and waited for her castmates to ask her why it looked so styled and perfect . . . and why she wasn't wearing the jeans and casual T-shirts she usually wore.

And she waited, and waited . . .

"Aren't you going to ask me why I can't get

meatballs all over this really cute outfit?" Sonny asked impatiently. "That you've never seen before?" she added. "That I'm *clearly* wearing for a reason?"

When no one responded, it became evident to Sonny that she'd have to take matters into her own hands.

"Okay, get off my back! I'll tell you," she said finally. "You know that entertainment show, *Tween Weekly TV*?"

Grady finally looked up from his sandwich. "Hosted by"—he wiggled his eyebrows and suavely lowered his voice—"Santiago Geraldo?"

Sonny beamed. *"Exactly!* They're doing a feature on me!" She couldn't contain her excitement. She clapped her hands and let out a squeal of delight. She could still hardly believe it. *Tween Weekly TV* was big-time!

Nico gave a nod of approval. "Very cool, Sonny," he said.

Tawni, meanwhile, didn't look that excited. "Let me guess," she said to Sonny, "it's one of those, 'let's follow the new girl around' stories?"

Sonny nodded. "It is!" she exclaimed.

Been there, done that, Tawni thought. She sighed and put down her sandwich. "Which brings us to Tawni tip number two." She wagged a warning finger at Sonny. "Watch what you say, because you don't want to look bad on camera."

Sonny gave her a curious look. She was already used to Tawni's know-it-all attitude. And Sonny had to admit that because Tawni had been on TV since, well, practically preschool, she *did* know a lot about show business. But Sonny also knew that Tawni still wasn't happy about having a new girl on the show. Tawni didn't like sharing the spotlight—at all!

"I'll be fine," Sonny assured her.

Tawni shrugged and went back to her lunch.

Just then, Sonny heard her stomach grumble.

"You sure you don't want some?" asked Grady, offering her a sandwich.

"Well, maybe just one little bite," said Sonny. A girl has to eat, she thought. She sat down, picked up a sandwich, and bit into it. *Mmm* . . . That was good, she thought. *And* messy. She looked around for an extra napkin . . . just as Santiago Geraldo walked in, along with his camera crew.

Sonny didn't need a mirror to know her mouth was covered with tomato sauce, and Santiago Geraldo didn't need a director to tell him to have his cameraman start rolling.

"One girl. One meatball," said the gossip-show host. He held his microphone in front of Sonny. "One quick thought?" he asked her.

Sonny waved as she tried to chew—and smile. "Hi, Mom," she mumbled, blushing.

Santiago smiled broadly. "Reporting for

9

Tween Weekly TV, I'm Santiago Geraldo." He wiggled his eyebrows in his trademark style, as Grady had done earlier. Sonny smiled sheepishly in the background. Well, that wasn't exactly the first impression she had planned on giving!

CHAPTER
2

Later that day, after Sonny had left with Santiago and his camera crew, and Tawni had gone off to fix her makeup, Grady turned on his computer and went straight to his favorite Web site.

"How's the online auction going?" Nico asked eagerly.

Grady sighed. "Zero bids, zero money," he replied.

"I don't get it," said Nico. "I thought the public loved to buy celebrity junk." He looked at the picture on-screen of the filthy old tube sock he'd worn in a recent sketch. He scratched his head. He'd been sure that offering something like *that* would make them twenty dollars, at least.

Grady looked at him and rolled his eyes. "I think the problem is we don't have the right celebrity," he said. "*Or* the right junk," he went on. He pointed to the auction page. "I *told* you to wash those socks."

"I did," Nico replied.

"Did you presoak?" asked Grady. "I told you to presoak."

Nico looked down. *Presoak?* He'd actually just worn them in the shower. "Okay, fine," he said. "I just want us to raise enough money to buy that new gaming system. . . ." He looked at Grady and sighed.

Grady knew just what Nico was talking about. "The Y-Box Four Thousand," he and Grady said in unison.

"Eighteen-button controllers . . ." Grady said.

"Forty gigabite graphics . . ." Nico added.

"Twelve hundred dollars . . ." continued Grady.

". . . That we don't have," Nico said, frowning.

Grady's shoulders slumped. They'd never make that kind of money selling dingy old tube socks, that was for sure! Then his eyes scanned the table, where he noticed Tawni's half-eaten meatball sandwich. "*Yet*," he suddenly said, giving his friend a small smile.

Nico nodded and picked up the sandwich. "Good idea," he said. "Eat first, think later."

"No!" Grady shouted.

Nico jumped back, startled. He looked at Grady. "You're right," he said after a minute. Then he reached for the bib that Grady was wearing around his neck.

"No!" Grady shouted again. "No bib. We're not *eating* it," he explained. "We're *selling* it." He carefully extracted the cold, soggy sandwich

13

from Nico's hands. "One authentic, half-eaten meatball sandwich, straight from the lips of TV celebrity Tawni Hart!" He could see the caption on the auction site already!

"Dude," said Nico, "there's lip gloss on it." A look of disgust came over his face, and he stood up to throw the sandwich away. But once again Grady stopped him.

"No!" Grady declared. "That's *Tawni* gloss! We can charge even more. To the Internet!" he commanded.

Nico shook his head. It was a crazy idea, but if it worked, the Y-Box Four Thousand could be theirs!

At the same time, across the studio lot, Santiago Geraldo had begun his interview with Sonny.

"So who *is* Sonny Munroe?" he asked as the camera started rolling. They were seated at a small table in the cafeteria. "And is she as nice

14

as everyone says she is?" he went on.

Sonny's face lit up. "Someone said I was nice?" she asked. "That's so *nice*! I should thank them. Maybe send some scented candles."

"See? Right there," said Santiago. "*Nice.*"

Sonny smiled shyly. Well, what could she say? She was just being herself. She couldn't help it.

Meanwhile, behind her, Chad Dylan Cooper, the star of *So Random!*'s rival show, *Mackenzie Falls*, was waiting in line for lunch with the rest of his castmates.

"Ugh, there's that clown from *Tween Weekly TV*," Chad groaned to one of his cast members. He gave a nod toward Santiago. "Ever since he did that story on me that made me look like a jerk, people think I look like a jerk. Do you think I'm a jerk?" he asked.

The girl opened her mouth to reply, but Chad kept on talking.

15

"Sure, I shoved a dog, but I had no choice," he told her. "It was slobbering all over me, and I shoved it away. And now I'm 'America's Most Hated Puppy Shover.'" He shook his head in disgust. "Man, I've got to figure out a way to make people think I'm nicer than I actually am. How?"

The girl tried to answer him, but Chad cut her off again.

"You're right. That's *brilliant*! This is a perfect opportunity," he said. "Thanks, I owe you one." Then he handed her his tray. "Pay for this, will ya?" And with that, he left the line and walked toward Sonny's table.

"You know, it really is a team effort at *So Random!*" Sonny was saying. She was really nervous . . . and rambling. "Because there is no *I* in 'team.' Of course, *team* spelled backwards is *meat*." She paused. "I'm sorry, what was the question?"

Santiago tried to stifle a yawn. "Where are you from?" he repeated.

Sonny clasped her hands excitedly and smiled widely. "Wisconsin. And there are two *I*'s in that!"

"Hey, Sonny, happy Meatball Monday," Chad said just then, walking up with a big grin on his face. "I brought you some extra napkins."

"Thanks, Chad," said Sonny, surprised. "That was oddly thoughtful of you." She still didn't know the star of *Mackenzie Falls* very well, but so far she'd gotten the impression that he wasn't much of a bring-you-extra-napkins kind of guy. At first, she had been totally starstruck by him, but after a few conversations and some 4-1-1 from her castmates, she'd realized he was pretty full of himself.

"Well, it never hurts to be nice," Chad said sweetly. He set the napkins in front of Sonny with a gallant flourish, then turned toward Santiago with a look of surprise. "Santiago, my man!" he exclaimed. "Didn't see you there. I'm so sorry!" He feigned even more surprise. "Are you guys in the middle of an interview?"

Sonny rolled her eyes. "What was your first clue?" she said sarcastically. "The interviewer or the camera?"

Chad completely ignored Sonny's comment and sat down next to her.

"Why don't you join us?" Sonny said, frowning. Wow! she thought. Tawni had always said Chad was a scene-stealer—but really, this was too much!

"Don't mind if I do," Chad replied.

"Hold up," Santiago interrupted. "So . . . nice girl from Wisconsin is tight with the Hollywood bad boy?" A look of surprise crossed his face.

"Well, I wouldn't say we were—" began Sonny.

"We're *very* good friends," interrupted Chad.

Sonny quickly shook her head. "Actually, we

18

can't stand each other," she admitted.

Chad chuckled and grinned at her fondly. "And this is the kind of fun we have every day," he told Santiago.

"Which, apparently, is starting today," Sonny said, bewildered.

Chad reached out and put his arm around her. "Isn't she adorable?" he said to the reporter. He gave Sonny a squeeze. "This is why Sonny is my favorite member of *So Random!*"

Sonny turned to him. "Really?" she asked in surprise.

"Yes, really," said Chad. "Santiago, you're lucky to get this interview. This girl is going places." He squeezed her shoulders one more time as he quickly checked his watch. "Speaking of . . . I have to go."

"Let me guess," said Santiago. "Got some dogs to shove?" He winked slyly.

Chad's face grew pale. "Yes . . ." he said,

thinking quickly. "Shoving the dogs toward bowls of food that I lovingly laid out for them. You know why? I love puppies." He gave Santiago a broad smile.

"Wow." Sonny scratched her head, genuinely surprised. "Compliments? Kindness? I'm impressed, Chad." Maybe he really isn't so bad after all, she thought.

"It's not about *me*, Sonny," Chad told her. "It's about the dogs." He turned to look straight at the camera. "It's just something I like to do that says 'Chad cares.'" He offered a wide smile for the camera, and then turned back around to Sonny. "Catch you later," he said with a wave.

"Well, that's a side of him I've never seen before," Sonny commented as she and Santiago watched him walk away.

The reporter crossed his arms and frowned. "That's because it's a side that doesn't *exist*," he said. He'd been around enough celebrities to

20

see through that kind of phony behavior.

"I don't know about that, Santiago," Sonny said slowly. "You know, when Chad wants to, he can be a really great guy."

"Interesting," said Santiago, nodding. He uncrossed his arms, held up his microphone, and looked straight into the camera. "Where will the story take us next?"

Sonny grinned. "My dressing room? You guys will love this!" She stood up and Santiago followed behind her.

"On my way to the dressing room"—the host wiggled his eyebrows—"I'm Santiago Geraldo."

Sonny smiled at the camera. "And *I'm* Sonny Munroe," she said with a wink.

CHAPTER
3

Sonny led Santiago and his crew to the dressing room she and Tawni shared. It was lavishly decorated—by Tawni, of course.

"Can you believe this?" Santiago said, taking in the faux leopard-skin rugs and chaise lounges. "A few weeks ago you were just a small-town girl living in Wisconsin."

"I know!" Sonny exclaimed. "I was just watching *So Random!* in my tiny bedroom, and now I'm sharing a dressing room with Tawni Hart."

22

"It's got to be exciting for you," Santiago remarked.

Sonny nodded heartily. "It is," she said.

"So what's a typical week for you and Tawni?" asked Santiago.

"Well . . ." Sonny began. "Mondays are great." She thought a little more about the way things tended to go with her costar. "Tuesdays are hard. Wednesdays are awkward. Thursdays are awkward because we're still getting over Wednesday. But Fridays—"

She stopped as there was a sudden knock on the dressing-room door. It opened, and in walked Chad holding an adorable yellow Labrador puppy in his arms.

He grinned. "Guess who?"

"What are *you* doing here?" asked Sonny incredulously. Chad was about the last person she expected to see in her dressing room!

"Well," he replied, "I said I'd 'catch you

later.'" Chad shrugged. "It's later, and I'm catching you."

"Okay . . ." said Sonny slowly. She didn't understand this at all. But as she'd learned from Tawni, stars were full of surprises. "So who's this?" she asked, reaching out to pat the head of the wide-eyed puppy. "Does this cute little guy have a name?"

Chad's face froze for an instant. "Uh . . ." His eyes darted around the room, finally landing on a half-eaten cupcake. "Yeah, it's Cupcake," he said quickly. "He's one of the hungry dogs that I feed." Then his eyes moved on to the cameraman, and to Santiago with his microphone. "The cameras are here?" he asked, acting extremely surprised. "Oh, my gosh. I've done it again." He shook his head in mock disbelief.

Sonny, meanwhile, was still petting the little puppy. "Can I hold him?" she asked Chad.

"Of course you can," he told her. Then he

practically dumped the dog into Sonny's arms and quickly backed away.

"He's so cute," Sonny said, giggling as the puppy began to lick her face.

"When I saw him I thought of you," said Chad.

Sonny stopped laughing for a moment. Had Chad Dylan Cooper just said something *nice* again? "That's a compliment, right?" she asked him.

"Of course," he said.

"Chad, I have to admit, I'm starting to like the new you," Sonny remarked. Obviously, she—and everyone else on *So Random!*—had judged him much too soon.

"It's not new, it's just me," Chad told her—or rather, told the camera. "People think they know me. But they don't." He smiled and winked.

Just then, the cameraman stopped filming and said something to Santiago.

"Guys, we're having a little problem with

the camera," Santiago told Chad and Sonny. He consulted with his partner some more. "Let's go to the truck," Santiago told him.

As soon as the interviewer and cameraman were out of sight, Chad grabbed the puppy.

"I have to go," he told Sonny.

"Wait, what are you doing?" she asked, confused. "You *just* got here."

"And now I'm *just* leaving," said Chad.

"Wait," said Sonny, a thought dawning on her. "You're not leaving because the camera broke?" She looked at Chad suspiciously. He looked down guiltily.

"Oh, my gosh! You're leaving because the camera broke!" Sonny cried. How could she have been so gullible? Chad hadn't wanted to catch her later. He'd wanted to appear on Santiago's show!

"No, that's not the only reason," Chad said quickly.

Sonny rolled her eyes. "Let me guess, the dog's a rental?" She laughed at her absurd joke. Chad, however, said nothing. "Oh, my gosh! The dog's a rental!" exclaimed Sonny. The whole feeding-hungry-dogs thing was just a big lie! Chad was worse—*much* worse—than she had ever thought!

"It's not that big of a deal. Look, you can rent anything in this town," Chad said, shrugging. "If I'd been getting bad press because I shoved an old lady, I would have rented an old lady."

"Wait a minute," Sonny said. "The cafeteria. The puppy. You 'catching me later.' You're just using me to make yourself look better!" Sonny's face reddened as she realized what his intentions had been all along. "I'm such an idiot," she said to herself.

"No, you're not," said Chad. "Look how fast you figured that out."

Sonny looked at him with disgust. "You're

unbelievable," she told him. "I guess I shouldn't be surprised that you used *me*. But to use this poor, sweet, defenseless dog . . ."

"I'm *not* using it for free," Chad said defensively. "This thing's costing me sixty bucks an hour."

Sonny clenched her fists. "You . . . You . . ." she stuttered as she struggled to find the right, biting words to say. "You poser!" she finally shouted. "You are the most shallow, self-absorbed, conceited jerk I've ever met! This is my room, and this is my interview, and"—she raised her leg—"this is my foot which is going to kick you in the butt if you don't get out of here!"

"Oh, man, this is great!" Santiago's voice boomed from the open dressing-room door.

Chad and Sonny both turned to find that the camera had been on the whole time! Santiago stood there, beaming.

"You were *filming* that?" asked Sonny, appalled. A sinking feeling washed over her.

"Oh, yes!" Santiago said excitedly.

"But I thought the camera broke!" Sonny cried, slightly panicked.

Santiago grinned. "This is a different camera."

"How much of that did you get?" Chad asked, suddenly concerned. After all, there had been those few minutes in which he had revealed his true motives.

"Just the part where she went all diva-crazy on you," said Santiago.

Chad's eyes lit up, then he instantly turned on a shower of fake tears. "And it hurts so much!" he sobbed. He turned to the puppy he was holding. "I'm sorry you had to see that, Cupcake," he told the dog.

Sonny watched in total shock as Chad hung his head and, still crying, held the puppy closer. Then he turned and walked off . . . followed by the cameraman and Santiago.

Sonny just stood there, speechless and utterly stunned. This was so wrong! Somehow, *Chad* had come out looking like the good guy, and she the bad one. She couldn't believe it! "This is the worst Meatball Monday ever," she groaned.

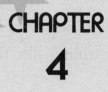

CHAPTER
4

Sonny showed up at the prop house the next day exhausted. She had been up all night thinking about *Tween Weekly TV* and how awful it was going to be. She had tried, of course, to tell herself it would be okay. She'd had a lot of *good* interview time with Santiago, after all. Maybe they wouldn't even air that last part with Chad! Then she remembered how excited Santiago had been when he caught her yelling at Chad.

Ugh. Yeah, right! she thought. But she was

going to try to be optimistic. Grady, Nico, and Tawni were in the prop house, and she didn't want them to know that she was nervous.

Grady and Nico, however, had other things on their mind . . . things like their latest online auction.

"Dude, we just made three hundred dollars on Tawni's half-eaten sandwich!" Grady whispered excitedly to Nico as he checked his computer one last time before rehearsal. Nico was about to give Grady a high five when Sonny suddenly screamed.

"No *way!*" she yelled, jumping in front of the TV.

Sure enough, there she was, shouting, "You are the most shallow, self-absorbed, conceited jerk I've ever met!"

And there was Chad, running out of the room with fake tears streaming down his face.

Then Santiago appeared on the screen,

standing outside the *So Random!* set doors. "An out-of-control diva, a broken heartthrob, and the innocent puppy caught in the middle. Where will this story lead? Reporting from the once animal-friendly set of *So Random!* . . . I'm Santiago Geraldo!"

Furious, Sonny raised the remote and furiously turned off the TV. So much for looking good on TV, she thought. "Out-of-control diva?!" she cried. "*I'm* an out-of-control diva?"

Tawni shook her head. "See, I'm an *in*-control diva," she explained to Sonny, "which is why this will never happen to me."

"This is so unfair," Sonny went on. "They didn't show everything," she said, pouting.

"You mean there's worse stuff?" asked Grady.

"*No!*" Sonny glared at him. "I mean they only showed the part that made me look bad."

"Well, you definitely looked bad," said Nico.

"Well, I know I sounded bad, but I did look pretty cute in my outfit, right?" she asked with a chuckle, trying to look on the bright side.

"Personally, I'm impressed," Tawni said approvingly. "I didn't know you had so much rage."

Sonny clenched her teeth. "I don't have rage!" she hissed.

All three of her castmates leaped back.

"Whatever you say," Grady said cautiously. He gave Sonny a nervous smile.

Nico winced. "Please don't hurt us."

Sonny sighed and turned away.

"Ooh! Ooh!" Tawni raised her arm and waved it. "I warned you to watch what you say or they could make you look bad," she gleefully reminded Sonny.

"Why do you sound so excited?" Sonny asked her.

Tawni clapped her hands. "Because this is the

34

part where I get to say I told you so!"

"Well, fine," Sonny grumbled. "Get it out of the way." She stood and waited for Tawni to rub it in.

But oddly, she didn't. "I'm not ready yet," Tawni explained. She took out her compact and fluffed up her hair. "I'm waiting for just the right moment." She touched up her makeup and practiced a few expressions in the mirror.

"Just say it, already!" Sonny cried.

Grady cowered behind Nico. "Would you stop provoking her?" he warned Tawni.

"Don't you see how explosive she is?" Nico added.

Sonny clenched her fists. "I'm *not* explosive!" she shouted.

And with that, Grady and Nico ran out of the room.

Sonny collapsed onto the sofa, drained. "This is *so* unfair! Chad hurt my feelings, then I blew my top, and now everybody thinks I'm the bad guy," she groaned.

Tawni snapped her compact shut and took a seat next to Sonny. "I know how to fix this," she said.

Sonny raised her eyebrows and turned to Tawni. Really? This she had to hear!

"But you have to say the magic words," Tawni went on.

Magic words? thought Sonny. She sighed. "You told me so?" she tried.

Tawni smiled and her eyes grew teary. "I did, didn't I?" she said fondly. She reached for a tissue and dabbed at her mascara. "I just love being right so much," she added with a little sniff.

She loudly blew her nose, then tossed the tissue in the trash can. "Come on," she told Sonny, taking her hand. They had work to do.

Grady and Nico, meanwhile, peered out

from the back of the prop house. Then, as soon as the girls were gone, they ran to the trash can. Grady held up a pair of tongs and Nico took out a plastic bag. Grady fished out Tawni's used tissue and dropped it into Nico's bag.

"To the Internet!" ordered Grady. They had some work to do, too!

CHAPTER 5

A short time later, Tawni and Sonny stood in their dressing room.

"What we're doing right now is called damage control," Tawni explained to Sonny. She had her hands on her hips and a huge grin on her face. "Now that you've become one of the most hated people in all of Hollywood—"

"You're really enjoying this, aren't you?" Sonny interrupted when she saw the gleeful smile on Tawni's face.

Tawni continued to grin as she turned on a small digital video recorder. "Yep," she said. "First, you need to hold a press conference where you'll admit you have an anger problem."

Sonny reached out and grabbed the camera from Tawni's hands. "I *don't* have an anger problem!" she cried.

Tawni cocked her head and gave Sonny a curious look. "You'll also admit to having a denial problem," she added.

Sonny rolled her eyes and headed for the door. "This is ridiculous," she told Tawni. "I'm not doing either of those things. I'm going down to the cafeteria and getting Chad to clear my name." As far as she could see, that was the only logical solution.

"The cafeteria?" said Tawni. She moved toward Sonny. "I'll come with."

Sonny turned back, startled. "To support me?" she asked.

"*Please*," said Tawni. She whisked past her. "It's Taquito Tuesday!"

Moments later, Grady and Nico, dressed in all black, poked their heads around the open door to the girls' dressing room.

"How's the coast?" asked Nico.

Grady scanned the room and took a step in. "Coast is clear," he reported.

They slipped in and headed straight for Tawni's makeup table. They eyed the cluttered surface like kids in a candy store, but Grady reminded Nico of the rules.

"Okay. So remember," he said, "we're only taking Tawni's *trash*." His eyes scanned the table. "Anything here look like trash?"

"Dude," Nico said, "I'm a boy. This is *all* trash to me." And with that, he pulled out a big, green garbage bag and swept everything into it.

Over in the cafeteria, Sonny and Tawni found Chad flaunting his appearance on *Tween Weekly TV*—and his new "nice guy" image.

"I'm not going to lie," he told the other *Mackenzie Falls* cast members gathered around him. "Sonny hurt me. But worse, she did it in front of my puppy. Do you know what it feels like to be talked to as if you're invisible?"

A girl beside him started to speak, but Chad cut her off.

"You know what? Don't answer that," he said, grabbing her hand. Then he continued his story.

"There he is," Sonny told Tawni as she started to walk toward him.

"There she is!" cried someone in the lunch line. "There's the girl who made Chad cry!"

And the next thing Sonny knew, she was being pelted with taquitos and refried beans amid a chorus of angry boos. She jumped back, and both she and Tawni grabbed trays to shield themselves from the food being thrown at them. Clearly, her reputation was even more damaged than she had imagined! Part of her wanted to run away. But another part told her that running away wasn't the answer.

"I'm going in," she announced to Tawni. "And I'm going to make him clear my name. Cover me!" she yelled. Then she rushed toward Chad's table as Tawni grabbed a basket of rolls off a tray and began throwing them at the cast members of *Mackenzie Falls*.

Sonny angrily walked up to Chad. "Chad—" she began.

Chad looked up at her and quickly grabbed the girl beside him by the hand. "Don't go anywhere," he told the girl. "I may need a witness."

Sonny took a deep breath. "I'm not going to yell," she told him calmly. She tried to smile—just as a roll hit her in the head.

42

Sonny tried to maintain her composure. "I'm not going to lose my temper," she went on—as another roll smacked into her.

"I just want to talk," she said—as one more roll came flying in.

Finally, Sonny spun around. "I thought you said you were going to cover me!" she screamed at Tawni, who was poised for another roll toss.

Tawni threw down the roll. She had done her best, but the cast of *Mackenzie Falls* was relentless! "Stop yelling at me!" she shouted. Then she turned and stormed out of the room.

Sonny rubbed her head and, with a deep breath, turned back toward Chad. "Can I have that seat?" she asked the girl next to him.

The girl nodded and pried Chad's hand off hers. She got up and hurried away, and Sonny took her seat.

"Wow, you're really working the diva thing,"

Chad told her with an approving nod.

"I'm not a diva, Chad," she replied, trying to keep her cool.

Chad shrugged. "I know that."

"Then tell that to Santiago," Sonny pleaded. "I want people to know me for who I am."

"And I want people to know me for who I'm *not*," Chad replied. "Look." He leaned in closer. "I like you, and I'm sorry the world doesn't know the real you."

"It's *your* fault," Sonny reminded him.

Chad cocked his head. "Is it, Sonny? Is it *really*?"

"Yes! It is! Really!" Sonny cried.

Chad frowned and checked his watch. "I have to go," he said quickly. He got up from the table, leaving his tray for someone else to clean up. "I told Santiago I was going to be building doghouses for homeless dogs tomorrow morning, so now I have to," he said with a look of disgust that showed just how unappealing the idea was to him.

"Wait, you build doghouses?" Sonny asked him.

"No." Chad shook his head. "But I know how to make myself look good in front of the camera!" He grinned, and satisfied, walked away.

Sonny, meanwhile, sat there fuming. How selfish could a person be?! Regardless of all the bad things she'd heard about Chad, she hadn't thought he would actually let her reputation be ruined just to improve his. But that's exactly what he was doing.

Just then a girl from the *Mackenzie Falls* cast returned to the table for her purse. Sonny turned to her. "How do you get through to someone who uses other people just to make himself look good?" she asked her.

The girl started to say something, but then Sonny suddenly had an idea.

45

"Fight fire with fire!" Sonny exclaimed, before the girl had a chance to answer Sonny's question. "That's it!" She jumped up from the table and gave the girl an impulsive hug. "You don't say much," she told her. "But you say a lot!"

CHAPTER
6

The next morning Chad, as he had promised, was at the park—along with Santiago and the *Tween Weekly TV* camera crew, a big, slobbery dog, and a pile of wood.

Chad stood proudly next to the woodpile as the camera rolled. "So, this is the park where, as you can see, I build my houses for homeless dogs," he explained. He reached down and picked up a hammer . . . then stared at it blankly, clearly not sure what to do next.

"Very nice. Very giving," said Santiago encouragingly. "Very—"

"Hey, Chad," said Sonny just then, walking up to him. She was wearing a tool belt and leading a big, cuddly dog of her own. "Wow! Is this the house you've been building for the homeless dog? Impressive!"

Both the host and Chad turned to stare at her, stunned.

"What are you doing?" Chad asked, clearly annoyed.

Sonny grinned and rubbed her dog's head. "Chompers and I just stopped by to bring you some extra nails," she replied sweetly. She reached into her tool belt and pulled out a handful of hardware to offer to him. "'We knew you were building doghouses! You know, never hurts to be nice," she added. Then she turned her attention to Santiago and—using a page from Chad's playbook—pretended to be completely surprised. "Santiago, my man!" she exclaimed. "I didn't see you there. Oh, my gosh," she went on. "Are you in the middle of an interview?" She shook her head apologetically. "I am *so* sorry."

Chad's face darkened as he took the nails from Sonny. "I know what you're doing," he whispered angrily to her.

"Do you, Chad? Do you *really*?" Sonny whispered back. "Okay, now let's get to building!" she announced loudly.

Santiago, meanwhile, was enjoying the drama. "Can an out-of-control diva be trusted with a hammer and nails?" he asked into the camera.

Sonny chuckled good-naturedly.

"Stay tuned," Santiago told his viewers.

Sonny and Chad both held up their hammers. The game was on!

Back in the *So Random!* prop house, Grady and

Nico were thoroughly enjoying their gigantic plasma TV and brand-new gamer chair. The flashy rings on Grady's fingers sparkled as he worked the controller.

"Uh, Grady," said Tawni, walking up behind him, "you wouldn't happen to know what happened to *everything* I own?" she asked suspiciously.

Grady gulped and kept his eyes on the sixty-inch screen in front of him. "Uh, no," he said.

"It just seems that every time I *lose* something, you suddenly *get* something," she went on, a little more insistently this time.

Grady bit his lip. "Uncanny coincidence. Un*canny*," he repeated. He held his breath, then let out a sigh as Tawni rolled her eyes and moved on.

Seconds later, Nico sped in on a jewel-encrusted scooter. A bulging garbage bag was draped heavily over his shoulder. "Dude, fire up the computer," he told Grady. "The Dumpster was filled with all this great Tawni trash." He had no clue that Tawni was in another corner of the room!

Grady frowned and nodded in Tawni's direction. "Why, Nico," he said stiffly, "I have *no* idea what you're talking about." He gave Nico a stern look.

"Oh . . . I *also* have no idea what I'm talking about . . ." Nico stammered when he caught Grady's drift.

Tawni put her hands on her hips and glared at both of them. But then she softened. "Guys, guys! It really doesn't matter whose fault it was," she said sweetly.

Grady and Nico breathed a sigh of relief.

"You're *both* going to pay!" Tawni cried angrily.

The boys looked at each other nervously. So much for their brilliant plan!

* * *

Meanwhile, Chad and Sonny were finding out that one of them was an expert at doghouse building, and the other . . . was not. Chad tried his best, but he couldn't build anything that would even stand up. Sonny, on the other hand, was a natural. Within a couple of hours, she had a series of sturdy doghouses lined up, *and* she was clearly having a great time with the dog she brought—while Chad could hardly bear to be anywhere near his.

"Well, we're two hours into it," Santiago reported. "Let's take a look at those houses."

"Oh, it's not about the houses, Santiago!" Sonny exclaimed. "It's all about the dogs. Right, Chad?" she said, giving Chad a wide smile.

"Right," said Chad, who was out of breath from all the construction.

"If it had been all about the houses, there would be no contest," Sonny continued, gesturing at her impressive—and structurally sound—doghouses.

"So is this all just a contest to you?" Santiago said quickly.

"What?" Sonny asked, thrown off guard. "Uh, no!"

"Out-of-control diva, also an overcompetitive diva," Santiago went on. "Reporting from *Tween Weekly TV*, I'm"—he wiggled his eyebrows—"Santiago Geraldo." Then he made a "cut" signal to his cameraman, and they were off.

Deflated, Sonny slumped against the big dog she had borrowed and let her hammer fall. "I give up," she said.

"Hey, you tried," Chad said cheerfully. "You *tried* to make me look bad, but you couldn't do it," he clarified. "You're just too nice. And I'm too good at *pretending* to be nice." He chuckled to himself.

Sonny shook her head. "I just thought I could

do to you what you did to me," she said. "But I can't play this game as well as you can." She sighed and looked at Chad. "I have to give you props," she told him.

Chad grinned. "Props accepted. The way I suckered you into letting me use *your* press to make *me* look better . . . I was brilliant," he declared, patting his own shoulder in admiration.

"Well, you've always done some of your best work on camera," Sonny said.

Chad chuckled, but then looked at her. "What do you mean?" he asked suspiciously.

"You're on camera." Sonny jumped up and pulled the cap she'd been wearing all morning off her head. "Smile into my hat," she said. She pointed her hidden-camera hat straight at Chad, catching the look of realization spreading slowly across his face.

"You didn't!" Chad cried.

"But I did." Sonny grinned. Then she brought

the hat close to her mouth. "Bad girl revealed to be good," she said into the hidden microphone. "Heartthrob revealed to be a *jerkthrob*. On her way to Santiago Geraldo"—she wiggled her eyebrows—"Sonny Munroe."

"Well played, Munroe," Chad said, shaking his head in defeat.

Sonny shrugged. "Props accepted." Then she turned off the camera and set it back on her head.

"We should hang out some time," Chad said approvingly.

Good try, but too late, Sonny thought as she crossed her arms. "The camera's off, Chad."

Then Chad surprised her. "I know," he said with a wink.

They shared a smile. Then . . . did Sonny suddenly feel her heart flutter? It couldn't be! Chad was cute, but Sonny knew by now that she'd be crazy to actually consider liking him. Besides, she had to get her video to *Tween*

Weekly TV before they aired the day's show. She waved to Chad, and they each set off in different directions.

By the afternoon, Sonny's name was cleared. And Chad was once again known as a puppy-shover.

Tawni was lounging in her dressing room with Grady and Nico on the floor beside her.

"Bite," she said. Grady held up a meatball sandwich. Tawni took a bite and chewed it slowly . . . *very* slowly. "Wipe," she declared. Nico reached over with a napkin and gently wiped her mouth.

"How much longer are we going to have to do this?" asked Grady wearily. His arm was getting tired, and he certainly wasn't making any money off this.

Tawni ignored his question and ordered up another "bite" and "wipe" instead.

"I wouldn't complain," Nico told Grady.

"She could make this a lot worse."

"I can't imagine how," said Grady, shaking his head. Then immediately, he wished he hadn't.

Tawni chewed and swallowed. She smiled and coolly said, "Floss."

PART
TWO

Part 1

"*Tween Weekly TV* is doing a feature on me!"
Sonny excitedly told her castmates.

Grady had a brilliant idea on how to make money:
sell Tawni's meatball sub online!

"Sonny is my favorite member of *So Random!*,"
Chad told the reporter for *Tween Weekly TV.*

"You're leaving because the camera broke!"
Sonny shouted.

"We just made three hundred dollars on Tawni's half-eaten sandwich," Grady said in awe.

The cast of *So Random!* watched in shock as Sonny yelled at Chad on TV!

"You're on camera," Sonny told Chad after he
admitted he'd tricked her.

Tawni couldn't believe that Nico and Grady had
been selling her things online!

Part 2

Tawni and Sonny's "Check It Out Girls" comedy skit was a hit!

When Nico told Zora he wanted to impress a girl, she offered to rent him her pet snake.

While Tawni admired herself in the mirror, Sonny hit the books. She *had* to pass her math test.

"I'm a cheater!" Sonny cried.

The producer of *So Random!* told Tawni and Sonny
that they were off the show until they both
passed their test!

Nico jumped into Grady's arms. The snake they
had ordered was scary!

"Grade our tests faster!" Tawni pleaded to her
math teacher.

Since they had passed their test, Tawni and
Sonny were back on the show!

CHAPTER 1

Life was good for Sonny Munroe. She absolutely loved being a cast member of the popular sketch-comedy show *So Random!* And every day just seemed to get better than the last. Even working with Tawni Hart was getting easier, and the comedy sketches, she had to admit, were funnier than ever, especially now that Sonny was even getting to write some! In fact, she and Tawni had actually written a skit together. It was called "Check It Out Girls," and it was about two supermarket checkout girls with . . . unique attitudes. Sonny and Tawni both agreed that it was sure to be a hit.

"Places, everyone! Places, everyone!" Marshall Pike, *So Random!*'s executive producer, shouted on the last day of rehearsal. "This is the final rehearsal for the 'Check It Out Girls' sketch."

Sonny looked down at her costume—a Hawaiian shirt and flowery hair clip—one more time and took her mark as the lights came on and the theme music started to play.

"And . . . action!" Marshall announced.

"So check it out," Sonny said, "yesterday I got a manicure." She held up her hands for Tawni to see. "Check it out."

"Ooh, check those out," said Tawni appreciatively. "Check *you* out."

Sonny nodded. "Right?" she said.

Just then, their castmate Nico Harris walked up to them, carrying a basket full of groceries.

"Excuse me, can you check me out?" he asked them politely.

"Sure," Sonny and Tawni said in unison. Then they surveyed what he was wearing.

"Check out his vest," said Sonny.

"His *vest*? Check out his boots," said Tawni.

"His *boots*? Check out his hair," Sonny went on.

"Uh, I want you check out my *items*," Nico told them.

"Check out your items?" said Sonny. She turned to Tawni. "Check out his *attitude*."

"His *attitude*?" Tawni replied, waving her hand. "Check out his *breath*."

"You know what? Forget it," Nico snapped. He slammed down his basket and stomped away. Just then, their castmate Grady Mitchell stepped up with a basket of his own.

"Excuse me, how about checking out my groceries?" he asked.

"Sure," Sonny and Tawni answered.

Sonny peered into his basket. "Check out his cereal," she said.

Tawni reached in and pulled out a sandwich. "Check out his panini," she said.

"All right, drop the panini. Give me all your money," Grady said, giving the girls a threatening look and narrowing his eyes at them.

Sonny made a face at him. "Check out the greedy panini guy," she told Tawni. Then she continued: "Check out his *jacket*," she said.

"Check out *my* jacket," Tawni told her. She reached under the register and pulled out a coat.

"Oh, my gosh! Check it out!" Sonny exclaimed, reaching down and pulling out a jacket of her own. "I have the same jacket!"

Grady frowned. "I'm trying to rob you here!" he shouted at them.

"Check out Mr. Pushy," said Tawni, nodding toward him.

Sonny looked him up and down. "Check out Mr. Pushy's pants," she said.

"His *pants*?" Tawni asked. "Check out Mr. Pushy's—"

"Oh, forget it," Grady groaned. He turned and stormed off as the girls watched him go. Sonny and Tawni looked at each other and grinned.

"Check it out," said Sonny. "He was kind of cute."

"Check *you* out," added Tawni. "He was a robber."

"Not a good one," Sonny commented.

"Right." Tawni nodded. "Maybe he'll come back tomorrow."

"Ooh!" Sonny exclaimed. "Then we can *re*-check him out." She gave Tawni a hopeful look. "Checkout dance?" she asked.

"Checkout dance," Tawni said, nodding enthusiastically.

65

Then the lights dimmed, a spotlight shone down, and dance music started blaring as the girls danced.

"And . . . cut!" called Marshall.

Sonny and Tawni both started laughing and walked across the stage toward Marshall. They were really happy with how the skit had turned out.

"Girls, that was great," Marshall told them. He put a hand on each of their shoulders. "I love that sketch! I see big things for these characters. *Big!* You can put those girls anywhere, and they'd be hilarious."

"*Really?*" came a prim voice from behind them. "Well, let's put them in class and see how hilarious they are."

Sonny and Tawni turned to see Ms. Bitterman, their on-set tutor, walking up to them. She was carrying a pile of textbooks, which she promptly handed to the girls.

"Check out our teacher, Ms. Bitterman," Sonny joked.

Ms. Bitterman gave Sonny a stern look. She took her teaching duties *very* seriously.

Sonny gave her teacher a weak smile. "Check *me* out heading off to class," she said quickly. And with a nod to her producer, that's exactly what she did.

CHAPTER
2

Later that morning, in their classroom in a corner of the *So Random!* studio, Sonny and Tawni sat side by side at a pair of desks in the back of the room. In the front stood Ms. Bitterman, writing equations on the blackboard.

"So you need to think of a trapezoid as six separate triangles . . ." Ms. Bitterman was telling the class.

As usual, only Zora Lancaster, the youngest member of the *So Random!* cast, was listening.

"That sketch was awesome," Sonny whispered to Tawni. She knew how much Ms. Bitterman disliked her students talking in class. But Sonny was so excited, she just couldn't keep it to herself.

"Calm down," Tawni whispered back. "It was just a dress rehearsal."

"Yeah, but didn't you hear Marshall?" Sonny said. "He sees big things for the 'Check It Out Girls.'" She held up her palm for a high five. "Come on, up top."

But Tawni just rolled her eyes. "I don't high-five, I don't fist bump, I don't peace out, and I definitely do *not* raise the roof," she explained coolly.

"Well, do you pay attention in class?" interrupted Ms. Bitterman, who had heard the girls whispering. She peered at them over her glasses. She was clearly annoyed. "Why don't you take a shot at that, ladies?" she said.

"Sorry, Ms. Bitterman," Sonny and Tawni muttered together.

"We're just really excited about our sketch," Sonny tried to explain. "I think I even saw you laughing," she pointed out.

"That's impossible!" snapped Ms. Bitterman. "I haven't laughed since I got out of the navy."

She turned back to the blackboard just as the afternoon bell rang. "Ah, the sound of sweet relief," she said. "Don't forget," she warned the class as they rose to leave, "you've got a big geometry test coming up." She turned and pointed to each of them. "For everyone but Zora, that's circles and squares," she added.

Sonny sighed. She knew her teacher was being sarcastic, but she wished it *was* as simple as circles and squares!

"Who can think about that test?" she said to Tawni as they walked back to the soundstage. "All I can think about is our sketch. The 'Check

It Out Girls' don't just have to be working in a grocery store. They could be anywhere. They could be nurses," she said excitedly. She slipped quickly into character. "Check out that cute doctor," she cooed.

Tawni shook her head. "Scrubs make me look boxy."

"How about astronauts?" suggested Sonny. She grinned. "Check out that cute martian."

Tawni curled her lip and frowned. "Space suits make me look boxy."

Sonny sighed. Tawni wasn't getting it at all. "It doesn't matter *who* we play," Sonny told her. "The point is, this could lead to bigger things. 'Check It Out Girls' T-shirts, backpacks, lunch boxes . . ."

Tawni held up her hand. "Actually, lunch boxes—" she began.

"I know," sighed Sonny. "They make you look boxy."

71

But Tawni shook her head. "No, it's always been a dream of mine to be on a lunch box," she told Sonny. She got a far-off look in her eyes. "And to have my own line of shoes called 'Tawni Toes.'"

Sonny grinned. So she *did* get it! "I've always wanted to be a doll," she told Tawni. "You know, one of those talking dolls. When you pull the string, and it goes: 'Check it out.'" Her face lit up at the idea. "Ooh," she went on, "and the string could break, and then it'll go: 'Check it out check it out check it out . . .'" she said, mimicking a broken record.

"Fingers crossed it doesn't break," Tawni said. Then she shook her head and walked away.

Just then, Marshall walked up to Sonny. He was talking on the phone. "Looking forward to seeing you, too," he said. "Okay. Bye-bye." He closed his phone and narrowed his eyes at Sonny.

"That was your mother. She's on her way," he told Sonny.

Sonny's mouth dropped open. "My mother's coming?" That was news to her!

"This can't be good," said Marshall, going into red-alert mode. "Somebody! Anybody!" he called to the whole studio. "Listen to me. There's a mother on her way here right now, and you are to do everything in your power to prevent her from . . ."

He trailed off as Sonny raised her arm and pointed just over his shoulder. Marshall turned to see Sonny's mom, Connie Munroe, standing less than a foot away from him.

". . . standing there without a coffee and a Danish in her hand," Marshall finished quickly. He loosened his collar and forced a smile. "Connie!" he exclaimed, holding out his arms.

Sonny tried to smile, too. "Hey, Mom," she said. Her mom *never* came to the studio. They

73

had moved all the way from Wisconsin and Mrs. Munroe wasn't a fan of all the Hollywood attitudes. So her coming to the set on her own in the middle of the afternoon wasn't a good sign at all.

"So, Connie," Marshall went on amicably, "what brings you down?"

Connie considered the question. "Rainy days, sad movies . . ." Then her face became serious. "My daughter's math grades." She crossed her arms in front of her chest and fixed her eyes on Marshall, then Sonny. "We need to talk," she said to her daughter.

"About rainy days?" asked Sonny hopefully.

Her mom gave her a stern look.

"You two go," Marshall said, giving Sonny a little nudge. "It's a beautiful thing, those mother-daughter talks."

But Mrs. Munroe shook her head. "You too, Marshall," she told him.

Marshall sighed. "It's a beautiful thing, those mother-daughter-Marshall talks," he muttered.

He ushered Mrs. Munroe toward his office, and Sonny followed slowly behind them. Her math grades might have fallen, but she had no problem guessing how *this* was going to add up.

CHAPTER 3

While Mrs. Munroe, Marshall, and Sonny discussed the finer points of high-school math class, the rest of the *So Random!* cast found themselves with some free time. Tawni took advantage of the opportunity to touch up her makeup, while Grady and Nico, as usual, looked for something to eat. They cleaned out the doughnuts, then moved on to sandwiches, then each took an ice-cream bar. Then they found a pair of director's chairs near craft services and sat down.

Nico took a bite of his ice cream, then grinned and nudged Grady. "Look at that," he said.

"I know, man," said Grady, gazing admiringly at his own ice-cream bar. "It's perfect."

"Look at all that hair," Nico went on.

Grady looked at his bar more closely. "You got hair?" he asked. "I got toasty almonds."

Then Nico shook his head and pointed over to the buffet. "No, *her*," he said. "The girl who stood behind us in the 'Check It Out Girls' sketch."

Grady glanced over in the direction of the girl Nico was referring to. "Dude," he said, shaking his head, "she doesn't even know you exist."

"That's because she's only seen the back of me. Now if I could just get her to see the front of me," he said. Nico figured it was his boyish good looks and charming smile that girls liked. He just hoped this girl would like those things, too!

77

"If only we could make that happen . . ." Grady mused.

They were racking their brains when Zora walked up with something on her shoulder. But of course, since this was Zora, the *something* wasn't just *anything*—it was a real, live snake!

"Fellas," she said matter-of-factly, "I couldn't help but overhear your conversation. There's only one way for a guy like *you* to get a girl like *that*," she told Nico. Then she paused as the boys leaned forward. "Rent my snake." She grinned.

Nico shook his head and leaned back again. "Zora, what are you talking about?" he asked. She often came up with creative ideas, but this one made *no* sense to him. Not to mention, he wasn't a huge fan of giant snakes.

"Here's how it works," Zora explained. She pointed to Grady. "Toasty Almonds here takes the snake, scares the dame." Then she pointed to Nico. "Then Lover Boy swoops in, saves the day, and ends up with the girl of his dreams in those toothpicks he calls arms."

Grady nodded as Nico self-consciously looked at his biceps. "That's brilliant!" Grady exclaimed. "That's like taking a girl to a scary movie."

"Yeah," Nico agreed. "They get scared, we get to hold them." He eyed Zora's four-foot-long companion. "How much for your snake?"

"Bernie will run you eighty-five dollars," Zora said.

Both Grady and Nico's mouths dropped open. "What?!" Nico replied. "That's outrageous."

But as Nico's crush walked by, he sighed. "Pay the lady," he quickly told Grady.

Grady held up his hands. "Hold on a second." He eyed Zora and her snake. Then he rubbed his chin and leaned in toward Nico. "Why rent when we can *own*?" he asked slyly.

Nico considered the idea. Maybe Grady was right. For eighty-five dollars—or less—perhaps they could *buy* a snake just as good. "Yeah, yeah, good call," he agreed.

"No, *great* call," said Zora. She shook her head. "Because your plans always work out *fan*-tastic." She rolled her eyes and walked away.

"Just so I'm clear," Nico said to Grady, "we're buying a snake?"

Grady nodded. "We're buying a snake."

Meanwhile, in Marshall's office, Ms. Bitterman had joined the group.

"So, Sonny, do you know why we're here?" the teacher asked sternly. Then she looked around, confused. "Seriously, I need you to tell me. I honestly do not know. I'm completely lost."

Sonny's mother spoke up. "I'll tell you why we're here," she said. "Sonny, can you tell me what the first letter in 'disappointment' is?" she asked as she held up a test paper with a big red *D* on the top.

Sonny winced. Marshall tried to lighten the mood. "Well, at least she didn't 'fisappoint' you," he said to Mrs. Munroe with a chuckle. Getting no reaction, he tried to explain his attempt at a joke. "Fisappoint starts with an *F*, and that's worse than a *D*. . . ." His voice trailed off when he noticed that Mrs. Munroe did not look amused. "Sonny," he said, suddenly serious, "your mother asked you a question."

Sonny shrugged meekly. "Mom, you know I've never been good at math," she said.

"No," Mrs. Munroe said. "I know you've never been *great* at math, but I've never seen you do this badly."

"I'm not a miracle worker," added Ms. Bitterman.

Sonny sighed. Her mom was right. She *could* do better; she knew that. "I've been working really hard on my new sketch," she explained, "and I just didn't leave myself enough time to

81

study. But I know I can bring my grades up." She looked pleadingly at her mother.

"And she'll have that chance," Marshall said, nodding. "There's a big test coming up and I'm sure she'll do better."

Sonny grinned. "I promise," she said.

All eyes turned to Mrs. Munroe as Sonny, Marshall, and Ms. Bitterman waited to hear what she would say. Sonny crossed her fingers behind her back.

"Fine," Sonny's mother said finally. "*But*"— she looked hard at Sonny—"if the grade doesn't come up, you're not doing the show."

"What?!" gasped Sonny and Marshall at the same time. Where had *that* come from?

Sonny jumped up. "Mom, you can't do that. Not this week," she begged. "Tawni and I are finally getting along!"

"Sonny, we had an agreement," her mom reminded her. It was one they had made even before moving to Hollywood. "Grades first, show second."

"Mom . . . Mommy . . . Mother . . ." Sonny tried. "What do you say we just, I don't know, switch it up this week? Show first, grades second." She looked around the room eagerly. "Who's with me?" she asked.

Tentatively, Marshall raised his hand. Then, noticing the look on Mrs. Munroe's face, he moved to scratch his head instead. "Scratching," he squeaked, quickly putting his arm back down. "Not voting. Scratching," he added.

Mrs. Munroe then turned to glare at Sonny.

"Okay!" Sonny said enthusiastically. "That's one scratch, one scowl—" from Ms. Bitterman— "and one glare." She was trying to stay positive. "See? Come on, I'm good at math. Up top!" She held out her hand for a high five, but her mother didn't move a muscle. "Sitting down,"

Sonny said, as she obediently returned to her seat. Gee, couldn't a girl have any fun around here?

Sonny thought to herself for a moment. Well, I'll just have to ace my math test, that's all. How hard can it be?

CHAPTER 4

As soon as her mom left, Sonny ran to her dressing room to start studying. When she got there, Tawni was hanging out and reading a script. Sonny started to explain what had just happened.

"So you promised your mother and Marshall that you would study hard so you could pass your geometry test and not let them down . . ." Tawni began slowly.

"Yeah!" Sonny said proudly.

Tawni scowled. "You selfish girl! What about *me*?"

"What about *you*?" Sonny asked in shock.

"The name of the sketch is the 'Check It Out *Girls*,'" answered Tawni. "I can't do it *alone*," she complained.

Sonny couldn't help but smile. "Are you saying you need me?" she asked. She almost couldn't believe it.

"No," Tawni said flatly, quickly dashing Sonny's hopes. "I'm saying I already asked Marshall and *he* said I can't do it alone. You *have* to pass that test," she snapped.

Sonny frowned and turned back to her book. "I have to learn five chapters of geometry in one night," she grumbled. "So instead of freaking me out," she told Tawni, "why don't you help me?"

Tawni looked back at her and slowly began to smile. "You know what?" she said. "I will!" She crossed over to the table where Sonny was sitting and held up her hand. "Up top," she said.

Sonny grinned and reached up for a high five, but Tawni grabbed her hand instead. "Hey! What are you doing?" Sonny asked.

"I don't know what you call it in Wisconsin," Tawni said as she began to write out geometric formulas on Sonny's palm, "but here in America, we call it cheating."

Sonny quickly pulled her hand away. "Stop that! I'm not going to cheat!" she cried, appalled. "I've never cheated in my life."

Tawni glared at her. "You promised me lunch boxes," she said. "I've been promised lunch boxes before, and I'm not going down that dark road again."

Sonny shrank back, half afraid . . . but half hopeful as well. "So you *do* need me," she said.

Tawni was silent for a moment. "If I say I need

87

you, will it help you pass the test?" she asked cautiously.

"Maybe," said Sonny.

"Fine." Tawni sighed. "Then I need you. Okay? I need you, I need you, I need you. I need you more than a flower needs rain. And more than a balloon needs air. And more than you need a spray tan."

Sonny glanced at her arms and hands. "I need a spray tan?" she asked.

"More than a balloon needs air," Tawni confirmed, nodding.

Sonny frowned, then shrugged it off and wrapped her pale arms around Tawni. "You *do* need me!" she cried.

Tawni hugged her back . . . and continued to write on Sonny's arm.

"What are you doing?!" cried Sonny. "Stop that!" She pushed Tawni away. "I'm not going to cheat. I'm going to pass that test, and do you want to know why? Because I've got one of the greatest minds of our generation to help me."

Sonny walked over to the dressing-room door and opened it triumphantly. There stood Zora, hands on hips, looking like she was ready to conquer all.

Zora was more than happy to tutor Sonny, and the prop house, with its blackboard from a previous sketch, made a fine classroom.

"Okay, a hexagon is simply two trapezoids, one on top of the other," Zora explained as she drew a diagram for Sonny. Her snake, Bernie, slithered slowly around in a nearby terrarium.

Sonny took notes and nodded.

"Now, this is the area of a trapezoid," Zora went on, "and you can check your equation . . ."

Zora continued, but Sonny's mind began to wander. She started thinking about the comedy sketch instead of what Zora was explaining.

"Hello?!" said Zora, tapping her pointer on the blackboard impatiently. "What's your answer?"

"Oh, um . . . um . . ." Sonny stammered. She bit her lip.

Zora sighed. "Okay, let me try this another way. . . ." She found some toy foam blocks and began to build the shape. "A hexagon is made up of six triangles. So if you solve the area for one triangle, you'll be able to . . ." But once again, Sonny stopped paying attention.

"Focus!" yelled Zora. She tossed a foam block at Sonny's head.

"Ouch! Sorry," Sonny said. She shook the daydreams out of her head. "Just one more time. And try and keep it simple," she begged.

But after an hour of trying to get Sonny to understand geometry, Zora was losing hope. "You're never going to pass that test," she told Sonny. She reached into the terrarium and pulled out her snake. "Come on, Bernie," she said sadly. "I don't want you to see any more of this."

Sonny watched her go. Then she put her head in her hands, feeling defeated. What was she going to do?

She sat up and sighed deeply. "All right, I'll do it. I'll cheat."

CHAPTER 5

Sonny walked into math class the next morning with a nervous smile. "Good morning, everybody!" she called out, waving, and trying to act perfectly normal. The she suddenly remembered her note-covered hand and yanked it back instantly.

She took her seat next to Tawni, who looked over at Sonny with a knowing smile. "You better pass this," Tawni warned.

"Don't worry," whispered Sonny. "I got this."

Up toward the front of the room, Grady and Nico were discussing their own plans.

"What time is the snake getting here?" Nico asked Grady.

"The guys at Snakes for Less guaranteed delivery before lunch, or . . ." Grady began to say.

"Or what?" asked Nico anxiously.

"Or we get it after lunch," Grady said with a shrug. "Either way, we get a snake!"

Nico rolled his eyes just as Ms. Bitterman walked in carrying a large stack of test papers.

"Good morning, Ms. Bitterman," recited the class in unison.

Ms. Bitterman scowled. "Is it? Is it *really*?" Then she looked around the classroom. "Is everybody ready for the big geometry test?" she asked.

"Yes!" Sonny blurted out nervously. "*Completely* ready. Come on! Let's go!" She couldn't wait to get this over with.

93

"Wow," said the teacher as she began to hand out the tests. "Somebody's an eager cheater."

"I'm a *what*?!" Sonny cried in horror. Had she heard her teacher right?

"An eager beaver," Ms. Bitterman repeated.

"Oh, beaver, right." Sonny sighed. "I *am* an eager beaver." As well as a cheater, she thought glumly.

Ms. Bitterman handed Sonny her test and studied her face for a moment. Sonny felt her face redden.

"That talk with your mother must have really helped," Ms. Bitterman said.

"Yeah." Sonny gulped and used her test to fan herself. "Is it hot in here?" she asked.

"It is," Zora spoke up. "I'll turn down the cheater."

Sonny spun around to stare at her. Had Zora said what Sonny thought she had said? "*What*?!" gasped Sonny.

"I'll turn down the heater," Zora repeated. She frowned. "You just don't listen, do you?"

"Why do we all have to keep recheating ourselves?" asked Grady.

"*What?!*" cried Sonny.

"Repeating ourselves," Grady replied, looking at Sonny in confusion.

Sonny fanned herself faster, but she could feel the beads of sweat beginning to stream down the back of her shirt. Her ears were clearly playing tricks on her, but were they trying to tell her something, too? And what about her heart, which was starting to race at about a thousand beats per minute? Was her heart telling her something?

"Is that my heart cheating—I mean, beating?" she whispered to Tawni as Ms. Bitterman moved on.

"What are you talking about?" Tawni asked, looking at Sonny as if she were crazy.

"Okay, class," Ms. Bitterman announced. "You may now begin your—"

"I'm a cheater!" Sonny shouted as she jumped up from her seat. She held out her hands, which were now smeared with ink because the sweat had caused all her notes to run.

There. She had said it. She could breathe again. She tried not to look around the room, but she knew everyone was staring at her, stunned. Uh-oh, Sonny thought. What have I done?

CHAPTER
6

Ms. Bitterman cancelled the test—for then—and sent both Sonny and Tawni to Marshall's office right away.

"I'm very disappointed," their producer said, shaking his head.

"I am, too," said Tawni.

"In *both* of you," Marshall added. He looked at Sonny. "You for cheating."

Sonny winced. "*Almost* cheating," she corrected, smiling hopefully at Marshall.

But Marshall was still frowning. "And you"—he pointed to Tawni—"for telling her to almost cheat."

Tawni shook her head firmly. "No, I told her *to* cheat. She ruined it with the 'almost,'" she replied.

"Well, until both of you retake that test and pass it without cheating," Marshall told them, "you're off the show."

"*No!*" Sonny and Tawni cried in unison.

"What about the 'Check It Out Girls'?" asked Sonny.

Marshall tapped his fingers on his desk. "They'll be played by Grady and Nico," he replied.

Sonny and Tawni gasped while Grady and Nico—who were spying through Marshall's window—pumped their fists and high-fived each other.

"The 'Check It Out *Guys*'?" Tawni asked, appalled.

Marshall shook his head. "No, they're still girls," he said.

Instantly, Grady and Nico stopped cheering and looked at each other, confused.

But Sonny wasn't about to just hand over her hard-earned sketch. This just wasn't fair—to Tawni or to her. "You can't replace us," she told Marshall. "That's our sketch. We created those characters."

"Well, my mind is made up," Marshall said. "You're both off the show, and the decision is final."

"But Marshall—" Sonny begged.

"My decision is *final*," Marshall repeated, getting up and heading for the door. "This is very serious business. Now, if you'll excuse me, I have to get two boys fitted for wigs."

Before any wigs were fitted, however, Grady and Nico's snake arrived. They carried it out to the soundstage in a sack and looked around for the beautiful girl they had seen earlier.

"Look at her," sighed Nico, spotting her by a wardrobe rack. "She's so pretty. I can't wait to scare her."

"Okay, let's review the plan, shall we?" said Grady. "When she comes this way, I'll open the bag, releasing the snake. You will know the snake has been released when I yell out something like, 'The snake has been released.'"

Nico nodded. "All right. Then I open my arms wide and prepare for the catch of the day." He demonstrated how he would hold out his arms, then grinned and snapped them closed.

"This may be the most foolproof plan we've ever hatched," said Grady. Though that wasn't exactly saying much.

Then Nico turned back to the girl. "Here she comes!" he whispered to Grady.

Nico opened his arms and stood there as

Grady opened the bag, turned it over, and poured the snake out onto the floor.

"The snake has been released," announced Grady. "And it's *huge*!" he suddenly cried.

Grady and Nico both looked down at the snake in horror. Nico leaped into Grady's arms as the gigantic snake hissed and slithered away. And Nico was still in Grady's arms when the pretty girl walked by and gave them a very strange look.

"You said you ordered medium scary!" Nico shouted at Grady.

"Yeah! But they sent us extralarge terrifying!" Grady exclaimed.

Nico held on more tightly to Grady. "What are you doing, man? There's a snake on the loose!" he yelled. The boys looked at each other and shuddered. Still carrying Nico, Grady ran off in terror.

CHAPTER
7

It was by far one of the worst afternoons in Sonny's life. She and Tawni were in their dressing room, well aware that the show was going to start in less than an hour—without them.

"Hey, hey," Nico said, walking through the door. He and Grady were both in their preshow robes. "We just wanted to say we'll miss you guys out there tonight."

"And speaking of missing," added Grady, "have you seen a snake about"—he held out his

arms and stood next to Nico, who did the same—
"this big?"

Sonny shook her head. "No, we haven't," she told him.

"Okay, well, if you see it, don't scream," Nico said. "Remember, we're doing a show out there." He grinned and waved as he and Grady walked off.

"I can't believe this show is going to go on without us," Tawni grumbled. There hadn't been a single episode of *So Random!* without Tawni Hart since the show had begun!

"I can't believe I let everybody down," Sonny groaned. "My mom, Marshall, you. I feel terrible."

Tawni was not one for giving sympathy. She turned away from Sonny and looked in the mirror. "I never know how I feel unless I'm looking at myself," she said. She studied her reflection for a minute. "Apparently I feel terrible—*and* pretty."

"If I had just passed that test," Sonny went on, "we'd still be in the show doing the 'Check It Out Girls.'"

"And whose fault is that?" Tawni said bitterly.

Sonny shrugged. "Well, it was your idea. . . ."

"Which you said yes to," Tawni told her.

"Well, it was your pen . . ." Sonny went on.

"Which you used," Tawni replied.

"Well, it was your . . ." Sonny sighed. "I don't have a third one."

"Let's see how I feel about that," said Tawni. She turned back to her mirror. "Now I'm *right* and pretty." She smiled. "You know what I love about me?" she asked Sonny. "I'm always *something* and pretty."

Sonny shook her head. "You know, you think this is all about you, you, you," she told Tawni. "Well, we're equal partners in all of this."

"Hold on," said Tawni. "Are we talking about the sketch or the cheating?"

"I'm talking about both!" Sonny cried.

"It's not my fault you didn't study," Tawni replied.

Sonny groaned. Tawni was right, but she certainly wasn't helping! "You know, you're not the only one here who's bummed out," Sonny went on. "The whole world does *not* revolve around Tawni. The world's a sphere, and we're all points on its perimeter, which means we're all equidistant from the center!"

Tawni sat back and cocked her head. "Wait, are you insulting me with geometry?" she asked.

The idea hit Sonny, as well. "I think I am!" she replied, surprised.

"Insult me again," Tawni said.

Sonny thought for a moment. "You're a rhombus!" she cried.

"I'm a *what*?" asked Tawni.

"A parallelogram with four equal sides." Sonny beamed. "Huh. I actually know this stuff!

It must have sunk in while I was writing it all down on my hand."

Tawni grinned proudly. "With *my* pen."

Suddenly, Marshall's voice sounded over the studio speakers: "*So Random!* cast members please report to the stage. Grady, Nico, Zora . . . that's it."

The girls exchanged a look of panic. "Wait a minute," said Sonny. "Marshall said if we take this test and pass it, we're back on the show, right?"

Tawni nodded. "Right," she confirmed.

"And our sketch isn't until the end of the show . . ." Sonny went on.

"Right," Tawni said again, not really sure where Sonny was going with this.

"So we *could* take the test right now," Sonny continued.

Tawni began to nod more enthusiastically. "Yeah."

"And we could be on tonight's show!" Sonny exclaimed.

Sonny looked at Tawni. Tawni looked at Sonny. "Are you thinking what I'm thinking?" Sonny asked excitedly.

Tawni thought for a moment. "I am," she said. "Let's go!"

Sonny and Tawni grabbed each other's hands and ran to find their teacher. They didn't have a moment to waste!

CHAPTER 8

It wasn't hard to find Ms. Bitterman, and after a few minutes of convincing, she agreed to let Sonny and Tawni take their tests. In fact, Ms. Bitterman came as close as they'd ever seen to smiling when they asked her. All she wanted, really, was for her students to do well in her class.

Sonny and Tawni answered the questions as quickly as they could, then gave their papers to the teacher to grade.

"Hurry up," Tawni urged, hovering over Ms.

Bitterman. "Grade our tests faster."

"You act like I have somewhere else to go," said Ms. Bitterman. She wrote something on one of the tests, but then the point of her pencil broke. "Uh-oh," she said. "Hmmm . . ." She held the pencil up, then slipped it into the electric sharpener on her desk. She pulled it out, examined it, then slipped it in again.

Sonny and Tawni both groaned. This was taking forever!

Finally, Ms. Bitterman took out the pencil and dropped it in her pencil jar. "Tawni, Sonny," she said proudly, "congratulations . . ." But before she could finish her sentence and say "you both passed," the girls were gone.

Sonny and Tawni raced down the hall toward the doors of the soundstage just as they were about to close. They grabbed their "Check It Out Girls," shirts off the costume rack and quickly slipped them on.

"Check it out, we still have time!" Sonny exclaimed.

"Check it out, we're going to make it on the show," Tawni replied. But just then the doors *did* close! The red on-air light started blinking. There was no getting on the set now. Oh, no!

"No! Check it out! It's closed!" Sonny shouted, extremely disappointed. She heard the announcer's voice from inside. "Are you ready to get *So Random!*?" he shouted.

Then Sonny suddenly noticed a ladder. "I've got an idea!" she said excitedly. She pointed out the ladder to Tawni. "Come on! Hurry!" she exclaimed, and started to climb.

"Move it! Move it! Move it!" called Tawni, giving Sonny a nudge.

At last they both made it to the catwalk, high above the *So Random!* stage, and the live audience.

"Careful . . . Careful . . ." Sonny said as they

slowly made their way along the narrow walk-way. Below them, the stage curtain began to rise, and the "Check It Out Girls" theme song started to play.

Then the lights went up, and the audience applauded.

"Our theme music! Hurry!" Sonny urgently told Tawni.

Meanwhile, Grady and Nico walked out in their own "Check It Out Girls" wigs and costumes.

"So check this out," Grady said. "Yesterday I got a manicure." He showed his hands to Nico. "Check it out."

"Ooh," cooed Nico, "Check those out. Check *you* out."

Then Zora, dressed as a boy, walked up to the checkout counter with a basket. "Excuse me, can you check me out?" she asked, setting the basket down.

"Sure," Grady and Nico said in unison.

"Check out his shirt," Grady said.

"Check out his shoes," Nico added.

"Check out his ears—"

"Uh, I'm right here," Zora interrupted. "I want you to check out my items."

"Check out your items?" Grady said. He turned to Nico. "Check out his *attitude*."

"His attitude? Check out his *breath*," Nico said.

"You know what? Forget it," Zora said. She stormed away in a huff, and Nico's crush, the pretty extra, walked up behind her, also dressed as a guy.

"Excuse me, how about checking out my groceries?" the girl asked.

"Sure," Grady and Nico replied.

"Check out his cereal," Grady continued.

"Check out his tuna *panini*," Nico said.

Then the girl looked at them menacingly.

"All right, put down the panini and give me all your money."

"Check out the greedy panini guy," Grady told Nico. Then he continued: "Check out his jacket."

"Check out *my* jacket," Nico commented, reaching under the counter to pull it out.

"Check it out!" Grady exclaimed. "I've got the same jacket!" And he reached under his register to pull out the other one.

"I'm trying to rob you here," the girl reminded them.

"Check out Mr. Pushy," Nico said.

"Check out Mr. Pushy's pants," Grady added.

"His *pants*?" Grady said. "Check out Mr. Pushy's—"

"Oh, forget it!" the girl shouted. And off she stormed as well.

Suddenly the lights began to dim.

"Checkout dance?" Grady asked.

"Checkout dance," Nico said.

113

Just then, dance music came on, and the spotlight fell on Nico and Grady. The audience clapped and whooped with laughter. High up in the rafters, Sonny and Tawni were fuming.

"We're too late," Tawni muttered.

"Those are our laughs," Sonny said sadly.

"Now the sketch is going to become theirs, and we'll never get our lunch boxes. The thought of Grady and Nico doing our 'Check It Out Girls' moves sickens me," Tawni said.

Sonny looked at her in surprise. She couldn't believe how well she and Tawni were getting along.

"Well, you have to admit, we do make a really good team," she told Tawni. Losing the sketch had been hard, but maybe there was a bright side, Sonny thought. "We'll do other sketches together," she said. "I'm funny, you're always *something* and pretty—" She sighed and reached out to balance herself with one of the ropes hanging from the rafters. Then a strange look crossed her face. "Is it just me," she went on, "or is this rope really slimy?"

She turned toward her hand. Her mouth dropped open in horror as she realized that it wasn't a rope she was holding. It was a giant, hissing, eight-foot-long *snake*!

"*Ahhhh!*" she and Tawni both screamed.

Sonny frantically shook off the snake, sending it plummeting down to the stage.

Below, Grady and Nico were milking their "Check It Out" moment for all it was worth.

They were smiling and bowing when, suddenly, the snake landed on the floor in front of them. The boys screamed. Nico jumped into Grady's arms, and Grady quickly dashed off the set just as Sonny and Tawni ran in. The audience cheered wildly.

"Check out our break being over," Tawni said, improvising.

"Check out the snake," Sonny said.

"Ew, you check out the snake," Tawni said.

"No, *you* check out the snake," Sonny replied.

"No, *you* check out the snake," Tawni told her.

"Check out neither of us checking out the snake," Sonny said. She and Tawni both grinned and nodded.

"Checkout dance?" Tawni asked.

"Checkout dance!" Sonny cheered.

The "Check It Out Girls" theme music started again, and Sonny and Tawni rocked out as the audience jumped up and gave them a standing ovation. The girls smiled at each other. The sketch may not have been perfect, but somehow, it was just right.

Hollywood is calling!
Look for the next book in the
Sonny With A Chance series.

IT'S SHOWTIME

Adapted by Sarah Nathan

Based on the series created by Steve Marmel

Based on the episode, "Three's Not Company," Written by Amy Engelberg & Wendy Engelberg

The set of the *So Random!* television show was bustling with activity. The cast and crew were busy getting ready to shoot the first scene of the day in front of a live audience. Sonny Munroe stood in the wings, ready to hit the stage. She still had to pinch herself. She couldn't believe that she had landed a role on her absolute favorite variety show on TV. She had come a long way from her home in Wisconsin to Hollywood, California . . . and so far, the trip had proved to be well worth it. Life was good.

Grady Mitchell, one of Sonny's co-stars on the show, stood nearby, dressed in a jacket and tie. He had the first lines of the scene. In a deep announcer's voice, as if he were filming an infomercial, Grady spoke into the camera.

"Has this ever happened to you?" he asked, raising his eyebrows.

The spotlight shifted to Tawni Hart, dressed as a student. She was wearing a plaid skirt and her hair was in braids. Tawni was another one of Sonny's co-stars, though if it were up to Tawni, there would be *no* co-stars—it would be the *Tawni Show*. On cue, Sonny entered the stage, which was set up to look like a school, and followed Tawni down the hallway. Sonny was dressed in a black leather biker's jacket and black cap. Two girls were standing next to her.

"Hey, loser!" Sonny called out. "Give me your lunch money!" She put her hand on her hip and gave Tawni an intimidating stare.

Tawni handed Sonny the money and then quickly ran off. Sonny started to laugh.

The spotlight then returned to Grady. "Well, now it's time to get that bully off your back," he announced.

Tawni walked down the hall again, only this time she was carrying a large black backpack. Once again, Sonny approached Tawni.

"Hey, loser!" Sonny said again with a smirk on her face. "Give me your—"

But before Sonny could finish her sentence, something smacked her in the chin. It was a boxing glove that was attached to a spring arm in the backpack! Caught off balance from the force of the blow, Sonny fell back into her two friends.

"Ow!" Sonny moaned, rubbing her chin.

Tawni smiled and skipped away happily as the spotlight returned to Grady.

"Yes! It's the bully-proof backpack!" he exclaimed as the music cued up. Pointing to the backpack that was now displayed on a revolving table, Grady began to list the bag's assets. "Its patented cartoon-violence technology is guaranteed to stop even the meanest of bullies. Each backpack has three awesome settings! Body blow, jab, and speed bag!"

Grady faced the camera. In his best used-car salesman voice he stated, "Now you can ride the bus, eat lunch, or go to chess club without having your head shoved into a toilet."

Nico Harris, another member of the cast, was waiting for his cue to enter the scene. Wearing a vest and thick black glasses, he walked down the school-hallway set with his large bully-proof backpack and stopped at his locker. Sonny came rushing up behind him.

"Hey, smarty pants!" she taunted him. "Give me your—"

Nico pushed a button on his backpack. The giant red boxing glove came out and punched Sonny. She fell back into her castmates.

"Ow!" she moaned. She faced the camera. "When will I ever learn?"